Apex Predator

John Donnelly's plays include *Bone* (Royal Court Theatre), *Corporate Rock* (Nabokov/Latitude Festival), *Conversation #1* (The Factory/V&A/Latitude Festival/SGP), *Songs of Grace and Redemption* (Liminal Theatre/Theatre503), *Encourage the Others* (Almeida Lab), *Burning Bird* (Synergy/Unicorn Theatre), *The Knowledge* (Bush), a version of Anton Chekhov's *The Seagull* (Headlong), *The Pass* (Royal Court Theatre), a version of Molière's *Tartuffe* (National Theatre) and *A Series of Public Apologies (Following an Unfortunate Incident in the School Lavatories)* (National Theatre Connections).

by the same author from Faber

BONE
SONGS OF GRACE AND REDEMPTION
THE KNOWLEDGE
THE PASS

adaptations
THE SEAGULL (Chekhov)
TARTUFFE (Molière)

JOHN DONNELLY

Apex Predator

faber

First published in 2025
by Faber and Faber Limited
The Bindery, 51 Hatton Garden
London, EC1N 8HN

Typeset by Brighton Gray
Printed and bound in the UK by CPI Group (Ltd), Croydon CR0 4YY

All rights reserved
© John Donnelly, 2025

John Donnelly is hereby identified as author
of this work in accordance with Section 77 of the
Copyright, Designs and Patents Act 1988

All rights whatsoever in this work, amateur or professional,
are strictly reserved. Applications for permission for any use
whatsoever including performance rights must be made in
advance, prior to any such proposed use, to
Casarotto Ramsay & Associates, 3rd Floor, 7 Savoy Court, Strand,
London WC2R 0EX, 020 7287 4450

No performance may be given unless a licence
has first been obtained

This book is sold subject to the condition that it shall not,
by way of trade or otherwise, be lent, resold, hired out
or otherwise circulated without the publisher's prior consent
in any form of binding or cover other than that in which
it is published and without a similar condition including
this condition being imposed on the subsequent purchaser

A CIP record for this book
is available from the British Library

ISBN 978-0-571-39808-9

Printed and bound in the UK on FSC® certified paper in line with our continuing
commitment to ethical business practices, sustainability and the environment.
For further information see faber.co.uk/environmental-policy

Our authorised representative in the EU for product safety is
Easy Access System Europe, Mustamäe tee 50, 10621 Tallinn, Estonia
gpsr.requests@easproject.com

2 4 6 8 10 9 7 5 3 1

For Cillian and Frances

Thanks

Henny Finch
Joe Hill-Gibbins for his generosity and dramaturgy
Kara Fitzpatrick
Lisa Foster
Greg Ripley-Duggan for the show of faith
Roxana Silbert
Chris Campbell
Dinah Wood
Lily Levinson
Jodi Gray

and last but very much not least –
the inestimable Blanche McIntyre

Apex Predator was first performed at Hampstead Theatre, London, on 22 March 2025. The cast was as follows:

Victor/Man on Train/Doctor/Man in Park/Neighbour/ Gil Leander Deeny
Joe Bryan Dick
Mia Sophie Melville
Ana Laura Whitmore
Alfie Callum Knowelden, Lorcan Reilly

Director Blanche McIntyre
Designer Tom Piper
Lighting Designer Jack Knowles
Sound Designer Chris Shutt
Casting Director Annelie Powell CDG

Characters

(in order of appearance, adult ages are guidelines only)

Mia
late twenties/thirties

Joe
thirties

Isla
five months

Alfie
eleven

Ana

Victor
forties

Gil
thirties

Man on Train

Doctor

Man in Park

Neighbour

Man on Train, Doctor, Man in Park, Neighbour, and Gil may all be played by the actor who plays Victor

A real baby should not be used to play Isla

APEX PREDATOR

Notes

The play is set in London, the present

A blank line within a scene indicates
a pause or change of thought

An interval may occur between parts One and Two

One

Overground tube
  Mia with her baby Isla
  A man on a call on speakerphone

Man (*to Mia*) What did you say?
  What did you just say?

Mia I just asked if it needs to be so loud

Man Why you in my business? Mind your own business

Phone Someone chatting to you?

Man Some ignorant bitch sticking her fat face in

Mia I can hear you

Man Did I not tell you? Did I not tell you?
  Look at me when I'm talking to you

Phone (*laughter*) She still there? Is she?

Man You think I won't slap you 'cause you're holding a baby, I'll bang you out
  Don't look at them, they're not gonna help you
  (*Still to Mia*) Look away. Look away. Look away

Flat. Night
  Mia shuggles Isla. She is dressed for bed. Joe wears a coat for outside
  Music intrudes from the upstairs flat

Mia First sign of the end times, the absence of courtesy. No please or thank you, someone takes umbrage, next thing you know World War Three's broken out on public transport

Joe Anyone say anything?

Mia Oh yeah, there was a civil uprising, people fell over themselves to help me
  I come home, think maybe some peace and quiet, then this (*The music.*)
  Hell is other people's music

Joe If it bothers you that much, ask them to turn it down

Mia What, *Would you mind ever so slightly not behaving like total cunts?*

Joe I wouldn't put it quite like that

Mia How would you put it?

Joe *Would you turn your music down, please, I've got a baby?*

Mia Do you not think if you were reasonable enough to respond reasonably to a reasonable request you wouldn't be playing music at fuck-off o'clock in the first place?

Joe I'll talk to them

Mia I don't want friction with the neighbours

Joe What's the worst can happen?

Mia They chop us up, stuff our limbs down the drain

Joe Or they turn the music down

Mia It's not that far-fetched. Some kids fishing found another body in Limehouse

Joe And you reckon it's the neighbours?

Mia According to Mumsnet it was mutilated

Joe Don't read Mumsnet

Mia There's some very informed people on Mumsnet. Where you going?

Joe Upstairs, if I'm not back in half an hour, get Mumsnet on the case

Mia I said no! I'm here on my own with the kids

Joe What do you mean, on your own?

Mia You're never here – this stupid job

Joe The stupid job pays the rent

The music stops. Joe gestures, 'There you go'

Mia It'll start up again

Joe How's Isla, feeding any better?

Mia (*shakes head*) It's daggers. I tried formula again, she just sicks it up

Joe Anything in the freezer?

Mia The pump makes me feel like a weird robot

Joe She's sleeping though, that's one thing

Mia Only 'cause I'm jiggling about. If I stop she screams the house down. I got a core like a pole dancer and a back like a retired brickie

Joe What?

Mia You got that look

Joe What look?

Mia The one you get when you've stopped listening and you're just waiting for an appropriate moment in the conversation to leave

Joe I have to get back to work

Mia You're only just here

Joe I'd stay if I could

Mia Alfie got in trouble at school
   He bit Arlo

Joe Which one's Arlo?

Mia Curly hair, angelic face, mean little twat. Dad's a governor

Joe Gilet and a flatcap?

Mia Yeah

Joe What he bite Arlo for?

Mia Him and his mates were teasing him about the class gerbil

Joe Didn't know there was was a class gerbil

Mia They take turns to feed it, change its hay, they get reward points towards golden time
   There was a letter, they named it and everything, they had a vote

Joe What's it called?

Mia Taylor Swift. Seriously. Second choice was Voldemort. They're proper eccentric, ten-year-olds, they're like tech billionaires, you know, super bright but also total fucking idiots

Joe What's this got to do with Alfie?

Mia It was his turn to look after Taylor Swift Gerbil at break. He's fed her and that, he's stroking her and his teacher notices it's gone a bit quiet, so she looks up from whatever she's doing and there's Alfie holding Taylor and she's keeled over, dead. Heart attack

Joe How do they know it was a heart attack?

Mia Because of the autopsy the caretaker did – what else would it be, it's a gerbil, they drop dead if you sneeze, they're useless!

Joe It died on him. That's a bit traumatic

Mia Exactly, he should be having counselling, instead, next day at break, these kids start calling him a gerbil killer
The upshot is, he grabs Arlo, bites his arm and one of the playground assistants sees, but what they don't see is what led up to it. So when Alfie tells them about what they said, they say he's making it up. It's their word against his and

Joe Arlo's dad's a governor

Mia Head said if it happens again, Alfie's looking at an exclusion

Joe For defending himself, that's taking the piss

Mia Why should Alfie get the shit when he's the victim?
I'm going to talk to his new teacher about it, see what she's got to say for herself

Joe He's got a new teacher?

Mia Mrs Hedges has been off with stress since the first week of term

Joe What's the new one like?

Mia Well, she's –
She's –
That's so weird. I'm sure I met her but I can't remember the first thing about her. My brain

Joe Maybe she's just not very memorable. Sort of person who gets booted out of *Traitors* in the second week

Alfie enters. He wears a papier-mâché mask with cut-out eyeholes

Joe Hello mate. Were we being loud?

Mia Alfie, take the mask off

Joe Is that the one he made, let him wear it

Mia Alfie, mask

Joe Come on, take it off for your mum

Alfie takes off the mask. Normal-looking boy

Mummy said you had a rough day. Don't let them get to you. You're worth ten of them
 Go on, I'll be through in a sec

Alfie leaves

Mia He listens to you
 Says he wants to go vegan
 I hate relying on you
 You work such long hours

*Joe approaches Mia – for a moment, she thinks/hopes he's going to embrace her – then he takes Isla.
 He rocks her
 Mia stretches her back*

Another tooth came through. Feels like someone's had a go at my nipples with a Brillo pad
 My body's not my own. Still not had my period. Or a decent shit. It's been a year, got poos like Maltesers, my arsehole's like a diamond mine
 I could pass myself on the street and not know who I was

School
 Children's artwork on display, including masks
 Ana has her back to us, cleaning brushes. Mia holds Isla

Ana The Head mentioned an incident involving Alfie and some other boys. I'm not in Thursdays so I've had to get up to speed – I gather it's been resolved but it's not ideal, is it?

Ana turns, wiping her hands

Mia It's not on
 Alfie getting in trouble, it's not on. He didn't do anything wrong

Ana He did bite another boy

Mia He was provoked. Arlo and his mates were chanting stuff about the gerbil

Ana Even if that was the case

Mia It is the case

Ana It doesn't excuse a physical attack

Mia You're calling biting a physical attack?

Ana What else would you call it?

Mia Self-defence

Ana Biting is something animals do

Mia You're saying my son's an animal?

Ana Come on, you're twisting my words, that's ridiculous

Mia I'm ridiculous now

Ana I'm saying he'd do well to learn some self-control

Mia Maybe if you did your job properly and paid attention to what the bloody kids are up to he wouldn't need to

Ana Why are you so insistent on seeing Alfie as the victim in this?

Mia Because he is the victim!

Ana Well I'm starting to see where he gets that mentality from

That was inappropriate, I apologise
    I'm sorry, I've had a long day but that's no excuse

Mia It's fine

Ana No, it's unacceptable, I'm sorry

Mia No harm done

Mia starts shuggling Isla, who begins to grizzle, quietly at first

Ana When I heard about the biting thing, I went straight to the Head and said 'Look, this is completely out of character, I'm sure there's something more to it,' and she completely shut me down. Went on and on about Arlo being this model pupil who would never do something like that and I said to her, 'I'm not sure you'd be seeing this quite the same way if it wasn't for who Arlo's father is,' and it was like a minor explosion hit the room. Wouldn't stop about how lucky I am to have a job at all, especially a school like *this*, how I'm on thin ice because I'm temporary, she was threatening me is what she was doing, not in so many words but – and I'm ashamed to say this but I backed down and when you came in, all guns blazing, which I respect, I felt guilty. Alfie's one of my favourite pupils and not just because he's so gifted, I mean he's a lovely boy, the kind of boy you get into this for, there's a sensitivity to him, an intelligence. In truth I feel I let him down

Mia What do you mean, gifted?

Ana His artwork?
    You must have noticed

Mia He likes to draw. I left him in the library, he's drawing now, are you saying he's good?

Ana He's exceptional. No one's spoken to you about this?

Ana hands a drawing to Mia
Isla begins to cry. It becomes steadily more intrusive

There's a wonderful sense of movement, you see how the figures around the cot assert themselves. It's beautiful

Mia He did this?

Ana I have to say I was curious to meet you, does he get his ability from you?

Mia I don't think so

Ana With your permission, I'd like to give Alfie some extra art lessons after school and in lunch breaks. Free of charge

Mia Sorry, do you mind?

Ana Please

Mia struggles to latch Isla. She succeeds but it's painful

Mia They've got knives for teeth

Ana Isn't the detail incredible, the glint of light on the blade, it's advanced stuff

Mia They look like they want to hurt the baby

Ana Oh? I would have said they're protecting it. Interesting what you see, isn't it?
 See, how these masked figures are looking outside the frame at us, that is very sophisticated, you'd expect that from a much older child

Mia examines the drawing

I meant to ask, in class, we were talking about jobs and Alfie was saying – and I'm not reading anything into this – that his father does secret things in the night?

Mia Oh! He's in IT, but he's freelance and lately he's away a lot doing tech support for the police, I think there's some surveillance involved

Ana Wow! That sounds fun, what sort of things?

Mia He's not really allowed to say

Ana Of course, it must be so hush-hush, forgive me
   It's just often children draw things that, while not literally true, express something that maybe they don't fully understand but is on their mind

Mia You think Alfie might be trying to say something about his dad with these drawings?

Ana I'm just wondering out loud, that's all

Mia in some discomfort as Isla feeds

Teeth coming through?

Mia Yeah

Ana I know that phase. Can I help at all?

Mia Not unless you want to feed her

Ana I don't mind

Mia I don't have a bottle on me

Ana That's alright. It's up to you, of course

Mia No, she's – she's just finishing, actually

Mia finishes up feeding Isla. She delatches her

Ana Like I say, I'd love to give Alfie extra tuition. It's a real treat to have a pupil as talented and receptive as he is. And of course I'd keep an eye on him in terms of, you know, the other boys

Mia Sorry, when you said *I don't mind* what did you mean?

Ana As soon as it came out of my mouth, I knew I shouldn't have said it

Mia You meant breastfeed her?

Ana This is so embarrassing but my aunts and grandmother used to share the feeding, it's so normal to me, but I know it's not for most people

Mia I was just surprised is all

Ana I really didn't mean to offend you, I'm so sorry

Mia Oh no, really, it's fine

Ana And look, if you do want to go back to the Head about the incident with Arlo, I'll totally back you up

Mia Yeah, no, it's fine

Ana I feel I owe it to you

Mia Arlo's dad would just kick up a fuss, it'd make things worse, but thank you

Ana If it's any consolation I think Arlo will think twice about teasing Alfie again. Between us, it was a decent bite

A hiatus. Mia glances at the masks

The masks, we were doing a project on rituals in different cultures and how masks can be about revealing rather than concealing yourself, you know, they give you permission to be who you are. Alfie loved that idea –

At some point, Mia has picked up a mask

You're welcome to take one, that's the sample one I made

Mia (*declining*) You're alright

Alfie enters. He's holding a drawing, wearing his mask

Ana Alfie. Your mum and I were just talking about your art

Alfie hands his drawing to Ana

Oh, I love it. Yeah, I love it. This is your best one yet, show your mum

Alfie shows Mia

We were just talking about you doing some extra art, would you like that?

Alfie nods then quickly looks to Mia

If that's okay?

Mia Course

Ana picks up the first drawing she showed Mia

Ana These figures, we were wondering, are they protecting the baby?

He nods

Mia Who are they protecting the baby from?

Alfie looks to Ana

Ana It's alright, you can say

Alfie slowly points at Mia

Flat. Night
Mia (holding Isla), Joe
Mia pointing at Joe, as Alfie did at her

Mia Said he misunderstood the question, that he's done the drawing for me

Joe His listening's never been great

Mia I think he knew exactly what he was doing, little shit

Joe Fair play

Mia *What they protecting the baby from, Alfie?* Muggins here. Like I'm an emissary of Satan

Joe The art thing's good though, that he's talented

Mia Said he's exceptional, wants to give him extra lessons

Joe That's what you need, someone who believes in you. She sounds like good news, she really does

Mia Yeah, well, yeah

Joe You don't sound sure

Mia No, it's just, she said something a bit, I don't know, it was –
  She offered to breastfeed Isla

Joe No, she didn't

Mia Isla was crying so I fed her and I was obviously in some discomfort and Alfie's teacher said, 'Oh I can do that?' or something

Joe She would have meant the bottle

Mia That's what I thought, so I said I haven't got one and she was like, 'Oh that's okay'

Joe Are you sure she meant breastfeed?

Mia I checked! She said it was something her aunts and whatever did when she was growing up that it was normal for her

Joe What did you say?

Mia 'No!', obviously
  She looked mortified, she was so apologetic, I think she just said it

Joe I mean it is a thing. And when you think about it, we drink cow's milk

Mia Not straight out the fucking udder

Joe Do you think you should make a complaint?

Mia About the one teacher Alfie responds to? No thanks. She said she'd keep an eye on him, you know, I liked her, it was just that one thing

Joe No harm done, I suppose

Mia This is the drawing he did

Mia hands Joe the drawing. He peruses it

He was inside me once. Now he's got his whole own little interior world I can't access

Joe Yeah, nice

Joe hands the drawing back

Mia She said in class they were talking about what jobs people do and Alfie said you go out at night doing secret things

Joe Fucking hell, that sounds ominous. Did you say anything?

Mia I said you do IT for the police and there's surveillance involved and that's all I know

Joe Okay

Mia I think she was suggesting it might be something that's troubling Alfie

Joe Why would it be troubling him?

Mia It troubles me. And he's sensitive
  We don't know where you go at night, what you do

Joe I sit in a room with screens and headphones trying not to fart too ostentatiously

Mia It's the hours. Sometimes you're gone for days

Joe It's specialised, we've had this conversation

Mia 'Cause there's something about you since you been doing this job, and Alfie's doing these strange drawings, what am I supposed to think?

Joe Don't think anything, thinking's bad

Mia It's nothing to do with these bodies they found in the Thames, is it?

Joe It's nothing to do with that

Mia You promise?

Joe Don't ask me any more questions, you'll get me in trouble. If there's a data breach the first thing they do is ask you if you've told anyone in your family so you just don't talk about it, it's easier

Mia Sometimes I wonder if this job gives you a reason not to be with me
   I want to feel close to you
   I can put Isla in her cot

She steps towards him. He steps away but tries to disguise it

Joe I know the hours are a bit mad but that's why it pays. We can get a house with a garden, somewhere away from all this
   This isn't like when Alfie was born, is it?

Mia That was a one-off

Joe I worry about you being on your own with Isla all day

Mia I tried going to one of those mum's groups but it was full of mums
   People are so stressful

Joe Why don't you see the doctor? Get something to take the edge off

Mia Got more chance of getting a ticket for Glastonbury than a bloody doctor's appointment

D'you really have to go?

Alfie enters. He wears the mask. He has a wet patch on his groin

Flat. Night
Music from above
Mia shuggles Isla
A doctor enters. He sits as if in a GP's surgery. He makes notes

Doctor What keeps you awake?

Mia Noise from the flat above

Doctor Have you tried talking to your neighbours?

Mia You've not met them. Are you writing that down?

Doctor (*writes*) Avoids confrontation

Mia Seriously they're a nightmare

Doctor You have nightmares?

Mia I think I might be having one now. Don't write that down!

He writes

My baby won't feed

Doctor It could be connected with your cortisone levels. Babies are highly sensitive to stress

Mia I'm stressed because I can't sleep. I can't sleep because she won't sleep and she won't sleep because she can't feed

Doctor Have you tried breathing techniques, white noise, history podcasts?

Mia My mind drifts, I have random thoughts that keep me awake

Doctor Such as?

Mia Paying bills. Getting old. Bodily decay. Dying. Illness. What to watch on Netflix. Whether to cancel Netflix. Being irrelevant. Not having achieved anything in life. My future. My children's future. Impending climate catastrophe. Being caught in a terrorist attack. My son being the victim or perpetrator of a school massacre. Minor social transgressions I was involved in ten years ago

Doctor (*writes*) General anxiety. It says here you experienced some sort of episode after your first child was born?

Alfie appears wearing the mask. Mia rises when she sees him. The doctor addresses her as if she's still seated

Mia My mother and father had just died and I just felt a bit overwhelmed. A neighbour found me wandering about looking confused. They overreacted and the police got called, there was this misunderstanding I'd left Alfie alone but it was fifteen minutes, tops, it got blown up out of all proportion

Mia moves towards Alfie. He backs away. Then leaves

Doctor What about walking?

Mia At night? Have you met any women?

Doctor During the day. Sunlight and exercise might help regulate your body clock

Mia If you could just give me something to take the edge off –

Doctor Over-medication creates a whole new set of problems. Mental illness isn't simply a case of genetics or brain chemistry. Two people could experience exactly the same events at the same time and while one crumbles, the other rises to the challenge. Think of it as a kind of latent potential – within some, not everyone – that is only awakened when our genetic predisposition *interacts* with our physical environment. And in this case, unfortunately, makes you poorly

During the above, Mia lays Isla down in her buggy and leaves the apartment complex (with the buggy). Her path is blocked by people without faces. She is forced to negotiate them

But equally, what if there was something dormant inside you, that could empower you? Make you stronger, more able to cope with the rigours of life? Wouldn't that be a thing?

Park. Day
  Mia pushes Isla in a buggy. She sits on a bench
  A man appears. He seems perfectly normal. He sits on the bench – not right next to Mia – and ties his shoelace

Man Sorry have you got the time?

  She checks her phone

Mia Two p.m.

Man Thank you
  No one wears a watch any more, do they?
  How old?

Mia Five months

Man Great age
  Such a lovely park this. You see that line of trees with the curve like a woman's back, when the light catches those at this time of day . . . magical
  How old did you say?

Mia Five months

Man Well, you haven't lost your figure

Mia looks at him, confused, a little wary

Mia Thank you

Man Anyway, nice talking to you

Mia You too

The man stands as if to leave, stretches, then turns to face Mia and masturbates
   A second before she notices

Oh

One of her hands moves to her mouth in shock. Her other instinctively goes to the buggy. Apart from this, she is petrified. Trying not to look, but scared to fully avert her eyes

Man Look at me. Look at me

Ana appears

Ana Hey! Hey! Fuck off! Or I'll bite your tiny dick off. I mean it, I mean it!

Man Sluts!

The man runs off

Ana Are you okay?

Mia I couldn't move

Ana You were scared

Mia I don't know why I couldn't move

Mia bursts into tears

I couldn't move, Isla was there but I did nothing, I didn't do anything

Ana Hey, hey, you've done nothing wrong. You've done nothing wrong. Look at me. He's a pervert, okay? You did nothing wrong. Okay? Nothing wrong

Mia nods
Ana holds her

You're okay

Mia He had a wedding ring

Ana What?

Mia He had a fucking wedding ring
 A park, a fucking park, it's daytime, anyone could have showed up

Ana Cities make people feel invisible
 You're fine, just sit

Mia Do you think he'll come back?

Ana No, no

Mia Should you not be at school?

Ana It's Thursday, this is my day of calm

Mia You can't get away from it
 I came here to de-stress
 I think Alfie's dad's cheating on me. He goes away for days at a time. He won't come near me. I shouldn't be telling you this

Ana It's fine

Mia Oh god, this is so messy, I'm so sorry

Ana It goes no further
 Have you talked to Alfie's father about this?

Mia He'd just say I was being paranoid

Ana I don't know, you strike me as someone with pretty good instincts

Mia checks on Isla. Lifts her from the buggy

Mia Were you not scared? With that man? You didn't hesitate

Ana Fight or flight I suppose

Mia I just froze. When you said Alfie had a victim mentality

Ana I shouldn't have said that

Mia But I'm worried he does and he gets that from me! I wasn't always like this, I'm so anxious all the time

Ana Maybe you've just lost touch with the animal part of yourself

Mia That's one way of putting it

Mia about to set Isla on to feed

Ana Let me

Mia stares at Ana – who smiles back, holding her gaze
Mia hands Isla to Ana
While talking, Ana adjusts her top and sets Isla onto the latch. Isla feeds

The world wants you to think your instincts are strange or wrong – you're too weak or too angry or afraid or unreliable but you're none of those things. There's a strength within you. I felt it the first time we met. I used to be scared of the world too. But the world should be scared of you

Ana takes Isla off the latch and hands her back

Hungry little thing

Mia stares at Ana strangely. She looks down at Isla

Mia Oh gosh, I didn't nod off did I?

Ana Only for a moment

Mia Why are you so nice?

They hold eye contact
 Ana takes Mia's hand. She upturns her wrist and strokes it and her forearm
 Mia gently withdraws her hand

I need to be home for when Alfie's back from school

Mia settles Isla back in the buggy

You won't mention this?

Ana Course not
Give me your phone

Mia unlocks her phone, hands it to Ana. Ana enters her number

If you ever need a friend

A beat. Mia leaves. Ana watches. Then leaves herself

Flat. Night
 Mia, Isla. Music from above
 Isla cries. Mia shuggles her, trying to get her to sleep. She continues to cry. Mia paces, more and more frantic
 She goes upstairs with Isla
 Music louder
 She bangs on the door
 Bangs on it more
 Bangs on it more. The door opens
 Music LOUDER
 The neighbour stares at Mia

Mia Please could you turn the music down just a little bit

Neighbour Is it bothering you?

Mia It's quite loud. I've got a baby

Neighbour Okay

Mia Thank you, I really appreciate –

He doesn't wait for her to finish speaking before he closes the door
  The music goes quiet
  Mia returns to her flat
  Mia shuggles Isla
  The music starts up EVEN LOUDER than before
  Mia slumps against the wall
  She sobs uncontrollably, holding Isla who starts wailing

Flat
  Mia, Joe
  Mia in same position. Isla gone
  Joe stands by her
  No music. Mia wakes with a start

Mia Where's Isla?

Joe In her cot. You'd fallen asleep holding her

Mia The music, it's stopped. Oh my god, thank god, I thought I was going to go mad

Joe What were you doing on the floor?

Mia The music was so loud I couldn't think

Joe The music?

Mia I asked the guy to turn it down, he turned it up. I thought my head was going to explode. It must have kept the whole block awake

Joe I'll have a word with him

Mia There's no point, he won't listen

Joe If it's causing you to collapse on the floor I need to talk to him

Mia It didn't make me collapse, I was just tired

Joe You fell asleep with Isla in your arms. What if you'd rolled over on her?

Mia I'd have woken up! I'm not going to hurt her

Joe I'm going to go up

Mia I don't want you to

Joe Why don't you want me going up there?

Mia I told you, I don't want trouble. I'm here on my own. I've said this so many times
   What are you looking at me like that for?
   You think I'm making it up

Joe I didn't say that

Mia Why would I make it up, you've heard the music?

Joe One time, yeah and it was annoying and inconsiderate but when I went into the bedroom I could barely hear it. Like I don't think it's as big a thing as you're making out, like it doesn't explain why you're falling asleep on the floor
   Did the doctor give you any medication?

Mia No

Joe Did you actually see him?

Mia Yes
   Yes!
   Stop looking at me like I'm making this up

Joe Sometimes you get an idea in your head of something that is actually happening, then you take that idea and you run with it a bit –

Mia I'm not making this up

Joe – and you make it a bigger thing than it actually is

Mia You're gaslighting me

Joe Oh come on, that's an internet word

Mia Internet word! – this is what you – you do this, you undermine me

Joe You're so paranoid, you make everything about you

Mia Where do you go at night?

Joe To work, where else?

Mia Stop LYING to me!

Joe Calm down

Mia Oh my actual god –

Joe Okay, okay

Mia – do not tell me to calm down!

Joe I'm sorry, okay, wrong word

Mia And don't do that fucking voice

Joe What voice?

Mia *Okay, okay, okay, okay, I'm so calm, I'm so calm . . .*

Joe That's just my voice!

Mia *. . . What you getting all emotional for, it's a conversation?*

Joe Any chance you could pretend you're a fucking adult?

Mia You are a genius at pushing buttons, you know that?!

Joe I don't want to say calm down again but I think you should

Mia You're seeing someone, I know you are

Joe Oh Jesus, I'm out, I'm out

Mia I can tell when you're lying to me, when you come home, there's something clinging to you like you're dirty, I so much as try and touch you it's like you've been electrocuted!

Joe I'm tired, Mia, I'm just tired!

Mia I swear to god I am *this* close to doing something I regret!

Joe What do you mean by that?
What do you mean by *doing something you regret*?

Mia Something's going on, I can smell it. Tell me. Who is it?

Joe It's no one

Mia I need to know I'm not imagining things!
Please!
Please

Mia trembles with distress

Joe If you say anything to anyone, if anyone found out I told you this, we would both be in serious trouble. It could jeopardise the case, prosecutions, you understand?

Mia Yes

Joe You can't tell anyone

She nods

Remember when you asked me if this job was to do with the bodies in the Thames?

Mia I knew it was that. I knew it in my bones

Joe No, you didn't

Mia You just told me I was right!

Joe You were afraid it was that, doesn't mean you knew

Mia But I was right

Joe If you keep expecting the worst to happen, eventually it does, that doesn't mean you're thinking straight

Mia Even when I'm right, I'm not right!

Joe Do you want me to tell you or not?
   I monitor chatrooms. Not just chatrooms, messages, all sorts but mainly chatrooms

Mia What kind of chatrooms?

Joe When the bodies started showing up, at first the police thought it was a turf war, one gang sending a message to a rival gang, but what was being done to the bodies didn't fit any of the profiles

Mia What was happening to the bodies?

Joe They had no blood left in them. Like an animal had drained them, they'd been bitten and mauled, a couple of them the heads removed, there's no animal could have done that – it must have been people
   They got forensics onto it, checked databases, all of it, but there were no matches so eventually they wanted to know if there was any kind of online profile. WhatsApp or chatrooms

Mia Why would these people be using chatrooms?

Joe People who do stuff like this love to talk, they need to, it's stressful being a psycho. They brag. Share stories. And eventually we found stories containing information that hadn't been shared with the public. On encrypted forums – which is really where I come in – that are niche

Mia Niche?

Joe For vampires

Mia For what?

Joe Not actual vampires, obviously. People who describe themselves as that. It's a fantasy. But they really commit. Like Dungeons and Dragons, they create this world of insane detail, the most mundane things

Mia Like what?

Joe How to get a new passport when you're three hundred years old. How to pass your inheritance on to yourself by creating new identities. Pages and pages on climate change. We're their food source and we're heading towards extinction. They can eat animals but it ages them. They talk about feeling let down by humans. Others say it's the end times and it's sparking a feeding frenzy. They talk about how hard it is to meet people, how lonely it is to watch the people you care about grow old and die and however much you try you never get used to it. How not everyone can do it, it's in you or it's not, but then it has to be released in you

Mia How?

Joe Apparently you feed from another vampire after they've fed from you, then you sleep or die or something and come back to life

It's one of these lonely ones we think's responsible for the bodies

Mia How come this isn't in the news?

Joe It would start a bit of a fucking panic if people thought there were vampires running about

Mia So they are real?

Joe Course they're not! But they think they are and it amounts to the same thing

Some of it's laughable, but some of it . . .

And you've got to pretend you're one of them, 'cause if you just lurk on these forums, they find you out, you've got to offer up stuff. Build a character, it's like acting. That's why I come home and I can't be close to you, I feel tainted. You have to make yourself numb

Mia It can't just be you doing this. You must have support

Joe There was another person but she had to leave. They tried bringing someone else in but the tone was off, they were on to them straight away, we nearly had to abort the whole operation

Mia When you say you feel numb, you mean numb to me, don't you?

Joe To everything

Mia Alfie and Isla?

Joe It's not going to last forever this job. Okay? It won't

Mia Will you hold me?

She moves to him. He stops her

Joe The colleague who left . . . She was the only one I could talk to about all this. She was having problems in her marriage and we became quite close. Nothing happened but there was this one night something could have done. We decided we wouldn't act on it but she left soon after

Mia What am I supposed to do with that?

Joe I don't want to lie to you

Mia Are you still in touch with her?

Joe She moved away

Mia Are you still in touch?

Joe She thought that wasn't a good idea

Mia So you wanted to be
  Do you think about her?
  Do you think about her?

Joe Are you telling me you've never had a single thought about someone ever?

Mia Do you still think about her?

Joe Yes, of course I do
  Jesus, I'm being honest

Mia That's what you call what you're doing now? Honesty?

  If you saw me in a bar and you didn't know me, would you buy me a drink, brush my arm with your hand. Lock eyes with me. Ask me back to yours?

  All the violence in this city is nothing to what you do to me

Wapping. The shore, a pub close behind. Night
Mia, Ana sit on the shingle – Mia with a glass of wine

Ana At one time, this would have been the first view of London coming in from the Estuary. The Bridge. The Tower. Dockers unloading cargo. Seven hundred years there's been a pub here in some form or other

Mia How d'you know all this?

Ana I am obsessed with podcasts. The other day in the park, you know with the pervert, I was listening to one about Halley's Comet. The Babylonians wrote about it in the first century. It circles the solar system, showing its dirty little arse every seventy or eighty years

Mia Sounds lonely

Ana You're very perceptive

Mia I was actually okay at school, just had the confidence knocked out of me at uni. I kept waiting for my mind or horizons or whatever to be expanded but it all just seemed like a horrible competition, who was cleverest, who was loudest, who could do the most drugs?

She puts her hand up

I was tremendous at drugs, they suited me, I think they actually genuinely made me more fun until I short-circuited my brain and stopped going to lectures. I drifted. Right into Joe, Alfie's dad. I was sat cross-legged on the mud outside the jazz tent – Jesus Christ – at a shitty festival in Finsbury Park, having a fucking awful one, and he appeared like an angel in a red checked shirt, sat with me, held my hand till it passed. His eyes seemed so kind

And when I got pregnant, it was like I found myself – I remember so clearly, I'd found my purpose, I was one hundred per cent going to be the best mum, in my soul I knew it, then just before Alfie was born, my parents died, quite close together, and the walls sort of collapsed in on me

Being a mum's one of those things you're just sort of supposed to be good at like financial planning or playing pool but

I've failed at everything I've ever done, I'm not fishing, it's how it is, the dreams I had as a child were so vivid but when they faded what's left was fear

That arsehole in the park, weren't you scared?

Ana No

Mia I could never be like that

Ana You could

Mia You think everyone's got it in them?

Ana No, but I see it in you. Someone saw it in me once

Mia Someone you're close to?

Ana I was, for a time

Victor appears from the direction of the pub. He holds a drink. He is dressed expensively

Victor Beautiful night
Sorry, am I interrupting?

Ana Not at all

Ana gives Mia a look that says, 'Relax, we'll just have some fun.' Mia is amused by this

Victor Did I see you looking at me by the bar?

Mia I don't think so, no

Victor What a shame, I could have sworn you did. That's very much my loss

Ana I was looking at you

Victor Now you're just feeling sorry for me
May I buy you each a drink?

Ana Are you very rich?

Victor I hope that's not a problem

Ana Not for me

Mia It's fine by me

Victor Or – how about a drink at mine? I don't live far

Penthouse apartment. Balcony. Night
  Ana, Mia, Victor. Drinks
  Mia startled by the view

Mia This is insane, you can see all the way to the Heath

Victor Not bad, is it?

Ana Is that Kandinsky inside real?

Victor Uhh – I *hope* so

Ana How much did it set you back?

Victor I couldn't possibly tell you anything as vulgar as all that

Mia Oh, be vulgar!

Victor Alright. I'll whisper it. Come here

  He whispers into Mia's ear

Mia Oh my days, are you shitting me? Are you an arms dealer?

Victor An investor

Ana Investor in what?

Victor Pharmaceuticals, emerging tech, anything really

Mia Do you invest in the arts?

Victor (*wryly*) Extensively

Mia Have you got one of those chairs with your name on it?

Victor No, but I have the wing of a gallery with my name on it

  Ana perches on the balcony wall/rail – her legs hang over the apartment (i.e. safe) side

If you're restless, there's a pool, we could take a dip?

Mia There is zero chance of me getting in that pool

Victor It's heated and I have robes, be careful that's quite a drop
 So how do you two . . . ?

Mia She teaches my son

Victor Ha

Ana No, I actually do

Victor looks to them both

Victor Is this okay?

Ana If it's okay with you

Victor Of course

Mia Do you have kids?

Victor Three. Grown up

Ana Are you married?

Victor Is it a problem if I am?

Ana No

They look to Mia

Mia I might actually need to go

Ana mouths that Mia should stay

Victor I'm going to fetch myself another drink, freshen up
 If either of you aren't here when I come back, no hard feelings but whoever is . . . I suggest we enjoy ourselves

Ana What a fine idea

Victor heads inside

Mia This was a laugh, but I really need to go

Ana You can't leave me here on my own, besides – this view!

Ana swings her legs over the balcony wall/rail so they now hang on the outside, over the drop

Mia Could you not do that?

Ana I watched this city burn. I remember the fire reflected in the water

Mia Why don't you come back over this side?

Ana I once stood in half an inch of piss while a man called Burbage spoke lines so beautiful, they silenced the drunks

Mia Yeah, well I saw classic Sugababes line-up at the O2, can you get off that, you're making me nervous?

Ana How would you like to never be afraid again?

Mia Right now, I just want you to get off that rail

Ana Okay

Ana drops
   Mia screams
   Mia looks over the balcony
   Victor enters with a drink

Victor Where's your friend?

Mia points

Mia She jumped

Victor cranes over

Victor What do you mean, she jumped?

Mia She just fell

Mia is unable to speak

Victor Oh fuck this is bad. This is bad, this is really bad, oh fuck
   Okay, okay, okay, okay, okay, okay
   Okay, we can sort this, I know how to sort this

Ana enters

Ana Sort what?

Victor Jesus Christ you're so not funny. Fucking hell. Fucking hell. Fuck, fuck
Okay, wow, wow, seriously that's amazing. Fucking hell
That's – you were so convincing!
That's got the blood pumping
I wish I hadn't taken the Viagra now
So. You're both still here
Shall we uh – yeah

Victor approaches Ana

Victor You're very beautiful

Ana What a charming man you are

*She puts her arms around his neck
She strokes his face
Mia heads out*

Don't you want to know what happens?

*Mia stops
Victor moves to kiss Ana*

Don't move. Not a twitch. I'm going to do all the work

*Ana moves her face close to Victor's, perhaps brushing his face with her nose and lips without actually kissing him. She moves her mouth to his ear
Victor is unbelievably turned on
Ana puts her lips to Victor's neck, softly
She leans into his neck*

Victor Ow!

Victor holds his hand to his neck, shocked

What the fuck?

*Then realises he looks like a bit of a wuss, so he smiles
Ana has blood around her mouth*

Victor realises there is a lot of blood coming through his hand
He stares at Ana, horrified. He scurries back into the flat
Ana follows
Perhaps we hear a gasp and a cry
Mia considers her options but there's nowhere to go
After a time, Ana returns, bloody
She smiles at Mia
Mia is rooted to the spot

Mia Please. Please

Ana Sh sh sh sh sh

Ana exposes Mia's arm if it's not already exposed. Mia seems unable to resist
Ana puts her lips to Mia's arm. Ana brings Mia's arm to her cheek, revelling in the feel of it
Ana holds Mia's wrist to her mouth

Mia Please

Ana Tell me to stop and I'll stop

A moment

Two

Flat
　Joe, Mia
　Dressing, after sex

Joe I could eat a horse. I could eat a cow. Which is bigger, a cow or a horse?

Mia Depends on the cow

Joe And the horse. I've a massive bruise on my hip, what got into you, you were like a banshee?

Mia I'd had some sleep

Joe There's a glow around you. You're glowing, you got colour in your cheeks

Mia My period came

Joe How long's that been?

Mia Fourteen months. Had my first decent shit in a year. My body feels like it's my own again. Didn't even hear the neighbours, that's how well I slept

Joe Isla's feeding, that's got to help
　I said some stupid stuff. I've not been there for you. This job is coming to an end, when it does, we'll carve out a bit of space, look after ourselves, look after you

Mia Why d'you say the job's coming to an end? Are you close to finding the person doing these things?

Joe I can't say much but – I think so. They're getting careless. That's the thing with people like this, if they knew when to stop they wouldn't get caught but it's not in their nature
　How was your night out, you never said?

Mia I don't remember much about it

Joe Were you sick on yourself? I got up for a piss, the washing machine was on, you were passed out starkers on the bathroom floor, window wide open

Mia It was a big night I suppose

Joe Alfie's teacher said you tripped and landed on the corner of a low wall, that's how you got the cut

Mia What cut?

Joe The one on your wrist – that's healed fast

Mia When did she tell you this?

Joe She popped round the day after, check you were alright. You were sleeping, did I not tell you this?

Mia No

Ana enters

Joe I liked her. Chatty. Bit nosy actually, kept asking about my work

Ana Don't you mind working those kind of hours?

Joe now addresses Ana as if alone with her in the flat. He flirts

Joe I've always been a bit of a night owl

Ana You strike me as one

Joe What makes you say that?

Ana You've got a glint

Joe A glint – have I now? That sounds trouble

Mia Quite a long chat was it?

Joe I invited her in. Seemed rude not to. Alfie's doing a presentation on climate change. That'll be great for his confidence

Ana Tell Mia I was here. When you get a moment

Ana looks directly at Mia

Joe You okay? Look like you seen a ghost

Classroom
  Ana, Mia, Isla

Ana You've not been at pick up

Mia Alfie's a big boy, he can walk home on his own

Ana Are you avoiding me?

Mia No, I was – embarrassed about getting so drunk, I imagine I made a bit of a fool of myself but I don't really remember, I don't even know how I got home

Ana Yes you do

Mia My dreams

Ana They're not dreams

Mia I've been getting cravings

Ana Yes

Mia Food disgusts me. I shake. It passes but each time it's stronger

Ana It just takes a little adjustment. Like moving to a new city where you've yet to find the good restaurants

Mia Why have you done this to me?

Ana What did you think would happen when you came up to the penthouse?

Mia I'd planned on a couple of Martinis and a bit of flirting, not becoming the Lord of fucking Darkness

Ana I did it because you asked. Because I wanted to. Because I could
   You wouldn't believe how long I've waited to find someone like you

Mia Like me?

Ana Like us
   Don't you feel it, making your heart beat faster, the light burn brighter, you've never known the night so vivid, have you?

Mia No

Ana Once you've seen the world as we have, you can't unsee it

Mia I don't want this

Ana Why be scared of the world when the world should be scared of you?

Mia Did you give that speech to the Year Sixes?

Ana First day, their little faces!
   I'm leaving. I want you with me

Mia Where are you going?

Ana Somewhere quieter, I don't know, I've been a little careless

Mia What about Alfie and Isla?

Ana They would come, of course they would

Mia Would they be safe?

Ana Safer than they've ever been

Mia I'm not sure this is what I had in mind for my kids

Ana It just requires a rethink of priorities. How high is Joe on yours?

   Mia begins to shiver

Mia You weren't checking on me when you came to the flat, were you?
You were looking for him, weren't you, not me?

Ana I wanted to know who was hunting me. I found Alfie and I found you

Mia shakes. She begins to convulse

You need to feed

*Ana exposes her forearm. She holds it to Mia's mouth
Mia pushes it away*

Mia No

Ana It's okay

*Ana keeps her arm there. Eventually Mia grabs it and feeds
Ana closes her eyes, ecstatic as Mia feeds greedily*

There we are

*Alfie enters holding a sheet of paper
Ana withdraws her wrist, clamps it with her other hand
Mia turns away wiping her mouth*

Your mum's just had a little nosebleed. I was telling her about your presentation, your vision for a shared future

He shows her the paper covered with writing and doodles

Oh, Alfie. Everyone's going to be so impressed

Mia recovers

Mia Alfie, let's get you home

Ana Alfie

*Alfie turns
Ana nods at him
Mia ushers Alfie out, watched by Ana*

Flat

Alfie sleeping. Isla in her cot. The small light on in Alfie's room
The window is open
The light flickers off and on
Ana is in the room, watching over Alfie
Alfie sits up. Looks at Ana
The light flickers again
Ana has gone

Zoo
Mia (with Isla), Alfie
Alfie's mask tilted up on top of his head

Mia Used to come here all the time when you were small. The butterfly bit was your favourite. The pupae, one time we saw one hatch, you remember?
You need to talk to me
Arlo might have broken his arm
Did you mean to push him?

Alfie Will I still be able to do my presentation?

Mia That's what you care about?

Alfie Can I hold Isla?

A pause. Mia hands Isla to Alfie. He holds her lovingly

Mia Would you miss Dad if you never saw him again?

Alfie Why would I never see him again?

Mia No reason, I'm just asking

Alfie Yes

Mia Would you miss me?

Alfie Obviously

Mia Secondary school'll be better

Alfie I didn't push Arlo

Mia The school thinks you did

Alfie Arlo said he felt it and Josh said he saw but they're wrong

Mia Alfie, we have to tell the school it wasn't your fault

Alfie But it was my fault

Mia You just told me you didn't push him

Alfie I made him fall with my mind just like when I made Taylor Swift Gerbil die

Mia Alfie, that wasn't you, it just happened

Alfie I was holding her

Mia There were no marks, no bruises. It was a horrible coincidence that you were holding her, I promise you, that wasn't you

Alfie rests a hand on Isla's head

Alfie I was feeding her a bit of carrot with my hand resting gently on her head. I felt sleepy so I shut my eyes

He shuts his eyes

and I started to wonder what it would be like if Arlo wasn't around any more to bully me. And I thought and I thought and I thought so hard about how much I hated Arlo and when I opened my eyes, Taylor was dead

He opens his eyes

Then today on the climbing frame, Arlo was playing with Josh and I asked if I could play with them and Josh said, 'No – you're weird,' although he was only saying it 'cause

Arlo was saying it. And in my mind I told Arlo to fall and I could hear him and Josh laughing, then Arlo went quiet and he fell. He had a really funny look on his face like he didn't understand as much as he thought he did

Is he okay?

Mia Can you give me Isla back please, Alfie?

Alfie hands Isla back. She's fine

You cannot say things like that, people can't do things like that

Alfie I can

Mia That's a lie, don't lie!

Alfie Miss thinks I can. She said I can do things no one else can do. She says I have the potential to be very special indeed. She says I already am

Mia I don't want you seeing her any more

Alfie She's my teacher. You can't keep me off school, social services will want to know why

Mia No more extra art, you don't see her outside class

Alfie Why?

Mia Because I'm your mother

Alfie That's no reason

Mia It's the one I'm giving you

Alfie You're saying that 'cause you haven't got a reason

Mia The reason is she scares me

Alfie She said you'd say that. But she said it's really yourself you're scared of

Mia Doesn't even make sense

Alfie I'm scared of you

Mia No you're not
Why would you be scared of me?

Alfie Sometimes you look at me like you want to hurt me

Mia I would never hurt you – Alfie, I would never, ever hurt you

Alfie Even the wolves are scared of you
Before, when they were feeding, they stopped and growled at you and you stared back until one by one they lowered their heads and rested them on their paws. You were looking at them with that look you get, the one that scares me, the way you're looking at me now

Flat. Night
  Mia paces, shivering
  She takes milk from the fridge
  She drinks it
  She convulses
  She vomits up the milk
  Alfie enters, wearing his mask

Mia To your room. To your room, Alfie!

  Alfie leaves
  Mia staggers to her feet, shivering
  She leaves the flat

London streets. Night
  Mia shivering, staggering
  Gil enters

Gil Are you okay? Can I help, are you okay?

He moves towards her. She backs away

Are you okay?

Mia Leave me alone

Gil I'm not going to hurt you. You're shivering

Mia I said leave me alone!

Gil raises his hands – 'Okay.' Leaves

Wait. Come back

*She staggers into his arms, he catches her
She attempts to nuzzle his neck. He gently rebuffs her*

Gil Oh, no, you're okay, you're okay

Mia You're out very late

Gil I work in a bar just over there

She persists in trying to nuzzle his neck. He continues to repel her, a strange dance

Let's go back, we could call you an Uber

Mia Why don't we find somewhere quiet, the two of us?

Gil Come on, I'll get you a cab

Mia Don't you like me?

Gil I think you're lovely and I'm very flattered but I have a girlfriend and children. I'm sorry

Mia How old are your children?

Gil Two and four, come on, let's get you . . .

Mia pushes herself away from Gil. He's surprised

I'm not going to hurt you. You don't have to come near me but we'll get you a cab

Ana appears

Ana Mia, who's your new friend?

Gil You know her? I think your friend's overdone it. I was just trying to help

Ana She does this, she'll be fine once she gets some food in her

Mia staggers and collapses

Gil I think we should call an ambulance

Ana There's really no need

Gil I'd feel better if we did

He takes out his phone

Ana Come here

Mia Don't

Ana I said come here

Gil approaches Ana

Mia He has a family

Ana Don't look at her, look at me. Look at me. What's your name?

Gil Gil

Ana Let me tell you a secret, Gil. Come close, I'll whisper it

Gil leans in
 Ana holds his head in her hands and feeds from Gil's neck
 He gasps, collapses

Now you. Now you!

Mia refuses to feed
 She convulses
 Ana uncovers her forearm
 She holds Mia's head to it

Mia feeds
Ana closes her eyes

Ana That's enough

Ana tries to release Mia but Mia holds on. Ana has to force her off

That's enough!

Ana is weakened
Gil groans

Mia I don't want him to die

Ana It's too late for him

Mia What if we turn him, we could turn him so he's like us

Mia bites into her own wrist

Ana Mia. It won't work, Mia, Mia, it won't work

Mia holds her wrist to Gil's mouth

Mia See. He's feeding

Gil convulses violently
He vomits blood
He convulses spasmodically, agonisingly, then stops, still

Ana What did I tell you? What did I say? People like us aren't ten-a-penny, he can't take what you're giving him

Mia He had a family!

Ana All animals have families! You're like a carnivore who won't eat a dog
Look around you! There's no civilisation, morality is an illusion. There is a food chain and all that matters is whereabouts on it you are
You have to learn to feed yourself. Or the next time the craving comes, you might be with someone you love

Gil moans
 Ana feeds on him
 Mia leaves quickly

Flat
 Mia enters
 She takes a moment, exhausted
 Isla begins to cry, off
 Mia exits
 Mia returns with Isla
 Mia sets Isla onto the latch
 She feeds her, comfortably

Mia Sh sh sh sh

You're going to be strong aren't you? You're going to be strong?

Mia looks up as music starts from upstairs
 She feeds Isla a little more
 She detaches her
 Alfie enters wearing his mask

Hey

Mia moves towards Alfie
 He takes a step back

You're safe with me. Mummy's going to look after you

Alfie exits to bed
 Mia exits with Isla (to her cot)
 She returns without Isla
 She exits
 Music louder as she *approaches the upstairs flat and knocks on the door*
 She knocks again
 Again
 The door opens. The music becomes louder

Neighbour Yeah?

Mia I want to come in

Neighbour You taking the piss?

Mia You seem like you're having fun

Neighbour You want to join the party?

Mia Yeah

Neighbour I don't think so

Mia Why not?

Neighbour You seem like a nice person

Mia Oh, I'm really not a nice person

Neighbour You're saying you're not nice? You saying you're nasty. Is that it? You nasty?

Mia Invite me in and find out?

Neighbour Yeah. You can come in

Mia enters. The door closes
The music becomes LOUDER

Flat. Day
Mia enters to find Joe holding Isla. Mia fetches herself a glass of water

Mia Where's Alfie?

Joe At school. It's the afternoon
 You passed out again in the bathroom
 Alfie saw you. I'd just woken up, I was moving you, when he came in to use the toilet, I said to wait

Mia What did you tell him?

Joe That you're not feeling so well
I'm worried. You've been going quite hard lately. Everyone's allowed a blowout but it's Alfie's teacher, you know what I mean?

Mia I'm not going to see her any more

Joe I think that's a good idea
Okay

Joe begins to hand Isla to Mia

Mia Don't go to work

Joe I have to

Mia It's not safe

Joe I don't go near anything, I'm in a room

He hands Isla to her. He begins to leave

Mia She knows who you are
Ana. Alfie's teacher. She's who you're looking for

He sizes her up

Joe I'll be back as soon as I can, okay?

A beat. He begins to leave again

Mia That's why she was here the other day
We killed a man in a penthouse

Joe Yeah, I saw it on the news

Mia We did that. Well, Ana did. Then she turned me into a vampire, I forgot to say, she's a vampire. That's why you found me the way I did, my clothes were in the washing machine because they were covered in blood

Joe We've been through this before

Mia No

Joe When Alfie was a baby you left him on his own for two hours

Mia It was fifteen minutes, the neighbour overreacted

Joe It was two hours, and you were wandering the streets telling strangers big tech was out to get us through surveillance

Mia It is

Joe Not by planting chips in our brains!

Mia This is different

Joe How?

Mia 'Cause this time I'm right!
   I'm trying to keep you safe
   She's made me better, Joe, this is who I was meant to be, I can protect us

Joe From what?

Mia What do you think? The world! Once you start looking, it's everywhere

Joe What is?

Mia The violence in men's hearts. Not just men, not all men, but mostly

Joe There are violent people but it's not – it's not most people

Mia You don't see it?

Joe No – Mia –

Mia Smile, not smile, keys in hand, not in hand, don't make eye contact but be aware of your surroundings, mirror signal manoeuvre, it's like driving in traffic all the time, it's exhausting! I see it in you too sometimes, like you could hurt me. And I worry about Alfie

Joe No, no

Mia How he's going to turn out

Joe Don't bring Alfie into whatever *this* is, that's not fair

Mia I see his drawings, what kind of man he's going to be, I worry

Joe Everyone has tried to help you, Mia, everyone
   When you couldn't cope, I took time off work to look after Alfie

Mia Time off work to look after your own child, how exceptional

Joe My mum and dad offered to pay for childcare but you said no because the thought of someone else looking after your precious baby was too much to bear

Mia I'm not leaving Isla with some stranger

Joe There's always something, you push everyone away, but it's never you is it!

Mia You don't believe me

Joe There is no such thing as vampires

Mia But I am one

Joe I told you about people who – it's not even that they believe it themselves, it's some game they act out
   You're talking about Alfie's primary school teacher
   She does collage!
   This is my fault. I put too much pressure on you, this is too much, all this time on your own

Mia So noble, so understanding, such a good man, so patient so patient so patient. That's why you like me isn't it? I make you feel superior don't I? Well you're not, you're weak

Joe I can't do this any more, I love you but
   I need to stop talking or I might say something I regret

Mia Look at him, bursting with restraint

Joe When this job is done, we'll have a talk

Mia Yeah, a nice talk. Let's do that, nice chat

Joe I have to go
Can I trust you – with Isla?

Mia I'm her mother

Mia sets Isla on to feed

Sh sh sh sh

*He watches. He's satisfied
She shivers*

Joe You're shivering?
Are you're okay?

Mia I'm fine, it's nothing

Joe You're not fine, are you coming down with something?

He approaches her. Mia covers Isla's ears – she doesn't shout so much as hiss with violence

Mia Don't TOUCH ME! DON'T COME NEAR ME!

*Joe leaves
Mia shakes and convulses
The late-afternoon sun goes down*

School

Ana Has Mum not come for you?

Alfie, wearing his mask, shakes his head

Why don't we practise your presentation?

Alfie hands Ana his mask

> *Children's renderings of the end times, increasing in intensity and violence*
> *Simultaneously, Mia leaves her apartment complex carrying Isla*
> *Faceless figures outside in her way. She stops. They part, so she can pass*
> *She prowls the sunless city, pulling strangers from the street, towpaths, subways*
> *A rampage of blood, all while holding Isla*

Alfie The world's best scientists tell us that human beings have caused irretrievable damage to the planet. Anyone who thinks this is not happening right now is silly. The bees will die. Flowers and plant life shortly after. We have betrayed Mother Earth, now Mother Earth is angry and she will have her revenge

> *Mia emerges from the darkness, bloodied, feral, triumphant, holding Isla*

Oceans will boil. Skies blacken like a witch's fingernails as wars are fought. There will not be enough food and birds will peck out our eyes and swallow our shrivelled tongues like wriggly worms! Pay-for-hire mercenaries will drive families from their homes, forcing them to seek sanctuary in town halls and places of worship. Theatres and schools will become makeshift morgues. This will not just happen abroad but here and in places like Berkshire and New Malden. Lewisham and Rotherham. Kensal Rise, Sevenoaks and Dortmund. The Thames will flood. The dominance of humans has come to an end

> *Mia vanishes*

Once the humans are gone, the earth will flourish and the climate rebalance. New organisms will form, nicer than us. Now Year Four will sing a song about bees

> *Alfie exits*

Wapping. The shore
Mia, Ana. Ana with a bag whose contents we cannot see – from its bulk, it could plausibly contain a human head

Ana First view I had of the city, the first time I came. That's why I wanted you to see it, it reminds me of possibility

Mia Surprisingly sentimental, aren't you?

Ana I like to think of myself as romantic

Mia Were you really afraid once?

Ana You should have seen me. Cowering slip of a thing

Mia But not any more

Ana No. Not any more
You're not coming, are you?

Mia I came to say thank you

Ana You think it's gratitude I want?
We could do anything, go anywhere, and you want your tiny life in your poxy little flat. I taught you not to be afraid

Mia I'm not

Ana Then come with me

Mia This is my home

Ana You hate it here!

Mia I love this city, even the people, I do! It's the fear that I hate. I want to be in my home, with my children, just not afraid, that's how things should be. What's the point of *this* if you have to keep running away?

Ana I'm not sure you're understanding quite how many humans there are in this equation. They're hopeless, there's just a fuck of a lot of them. You know? It's easier this way, I promise you

Mia You're not running away from humans

Ana I'm running away from myself, is it?

Mia Yes

Ana Are you analysing me?

Mia Tell me I'm wrong

Ana You're not wrong. Which is annoying. It's obvious but still annoying

Mia Where would you even go? Are there places you haven't been before, I mean how does this lifestyle even work on a teacher's salary?

Ana I've other sources of income

Mia So what are you a teacher for?

Ana The pension's very good
   I genuinely like the job, not the marking, obviously but –
   Children only really see the present, which is handy if you want to take your mind off the future. Rolling away from you into eternity, like a threadbare carpet
   There's nothing for you here, nothing you can't bring with you
   Please. I don't know if I can do this alone any more
   After two hundred years of drifting, you woke me up
   Keep me company, will you?

Mia looks away briefly

You've outgrown me, is that it?

Mia You don't need to be unkind

Ana Says the woman with blood on her hands

Mia I'm sorry

Ana No, I am
   I wanted you to choose me like I chose you
   But I can't let you go. Not after waiting so long
   Come to me

Mia Don't do this

Ana I said come to me

Mia moves towards Ana

Mia You'd make me?

Ana You're leaving me with no choice

Ana strokes Mia's face with tenderness

Look at me. Look at me. You're with me, now

Mia On your knees

Slowly, Ana drops to her knees and prostrates herself before Mia
  Mia moves away, her back to Ana

You can get up now

Ana stands
  She backs away, overwhelmed

I like you. But lately you're stifling me

Mia begins to leave

Ana You've taken what you needed, now you're off? Is that it?

Mia Told you, you were sentimental

Ana Do you not want to know what's in the bag?

Mia stops – sees the bag

Did Joe mention sometimes the heads are separated from the bodies?
  Like popping the lid off

Mia Where are my children?

Ana At home, safe

Mia Where's Joe?

Mia picks up the bag
  Scared, she opens it
  She pulls out two masks and folders

Ana Alfie's artwork. And his mask. He left it at school

Mia How was his presentation?

Ana He rushed it a bit but mostly very good
The other mask is the one you liked. The one I made, if you want it

Mia begins to leave

You know the worst of it is I can't remember my children's faces. I thought the memory would never fade but it does
Could you live with that?
There it is. The rage I saw that first day
Keep telling yourself you're doing this for your children. I don't know if you even want anything. This is just who you are. Something you were born for

Mia Will I ever see you again?

Ana There's always time

Ana leaves

Flat. Night
  Mia enters
  She sets the bag containing Alfie's artwork down
  She takes the art out and the two masks
  She looks through the artwork
  She's deeply moved
  She nods to herself
  Alfie enters, holding Isla

Mia Hey baby

She takes a step towards him
  He takes a step back
  She stops

Sorry I missed your presentation. I hear you were the star of the show. You left your mask, Miss gave it to me to give to you
  She isn't going to be around any more. She had to move to a different school and she's so sorry but she wants you to know how special you are because you are. Both you and Isla are special. She gave me a mask, too
  It's weird when adults change. You're changing too, you can feel it can't you, in your brain and your gut and soon in your body, and that feeling is the start of you becoming a new you. There are so many different versions of all of us. Our job is to be the best one possible, the truest one. That's what happened to me and that's what I want for you too
  Miss gave me a gift to pass on to you, and for Isla. It will make you so strong and so brave and you won't ever need to be worried about anything again
  Do you like the sound of that?

Alfie nods

You'll have to trust me though, can you do that?
  Look me in the eye

Alfie nods

Precious boy

  Mia leads Alfie and Isla off
    A long while
    Perhaps we hear a small gasp
    Joe enters with a busy energy. He fetches himself water
    He sees Alfie's artwork
    He looks through it, smiles
    Mia enters, hands tucked into her armpits, shoulders hunched

Joe It's over
The job's done, it's over

Mia You found them, did you?

Joe That doesn't matter

Mia But did you find them?

Joe We think they left the country. All that matters is it's someone else's problem now

Mia But you know who it was?

Joe Mia. It was a man. Okay? It always is. There is physical evidence connecting him to the bodies, that's all you need to know

Mia All the bodies? Or just some of them

Joe I want to make things work, with you and Alfie and Isla, I really do, I really really do, but I don't know if that's –

Mia (*interrupting*) It's too late
I'm sorry. I had to keep them safe

Mia removes her bloody hands from her armpits. Shows them to Joe
Joe exits (into the bedroom)
Mia crosses to the surface/table and goes through a few of Alfie's drawings, carefully and with pride
Joe returns, ashen-faced, blood on his hands and shirt, consistent with having been in contact with bloodied bodies

I probably should have talked it through but you'd only have tried to stop me
Joe, this is a good thing. Any second now, they're going to come back, but stronger. It seems impossible, but they will. I did it too

She looks and waits

I don't know how long it takes exactly because obviously when it happens to you, you're not aware of it but I can't imagine it's that long
   And when they come back they'll be ready for the world, you know, at the top of the tree but – and this is important – I'm going to make sure they use that strength responsibly, for good. Especially Alfie, he'll be a role model and not a pretend role model like you, Joe. I know you think you're kind and a good person but for you kindness is just another form of control, isn't it? Making me think I'm not good enough, that I need you, well, I don't, not any more

Joe You have no idea how much I want to hurt you

Mia I'd like to see you try

Joe This isn't your fault, this isn't your fault, this isn't your fault

She looks towards the door that leads to the bedrooms

Mia Any second now, they'll be out. You'll see

Joe They're not coming out

Mia Any second. Any second

Joe They're not coming out, Mia!

Mia You just need a little patience
   The music, that's it! The music, there's no music
   I killed the neighbour. That's why there's no music. There's your proof, there!

Joe You killed the neighbour?

Mia I ate him, well, drank him, fed from him, I'm still getting to grips with the language

Joe Because you're a vampire?

Mia Yes!

Joe Because Alfie's primary school teacher turned you into one

Mia It's just what happened

Joe I asked him to turn it down. I went upstairs and told them to pack it in. That's why there's no music, Mia. Because I asked them to turn it down

Mia Well that must have been before I killed him 'cause I definitely killed him and I drank his blood
    I wouldn't forget that kind of thing

A terrible realisation

Oh god
    Oh god
    Oh god, what have I done?
    I never get anything right!
    My babies
    Isla
    Alfie
    His drawings, look at his artwork, look at it
    Look how good his drawings are

Joe I don't want to see his drawings

She picks them up. She tries to force them on him

Mia Look at them though

Joe I don't want to see them

Mia Look at them!

Joe I DON'T WANT HIS DRAWINGS, I WANT HIM! I WANT MY CHILDREN!

*He flings the drawings up in the air
    While he does this:
    Alfie enters wearing his mask, holding Isla, shuggling her gently. His arm is bloody. Isla is bloody
    Joe surveys the scattered drawings*

Mia sees Alfie first
She laughs with relief
Joe turns

Alfie

Joe instinctively steps towards Alfie, then stops abruptly
Mia calmly takes her mask and puts it on
Mia and Alfie both look at Joe
Alfie points at Joe